Honouring the BUFFALO
A Plains Cree Legend

ēwako ōma ohci paskwāwi-mostos kā-kistēyimiht
nēhiyaw-ācimowin

told by Ray Lavallee, Wisdom Keeper
written by Judith Silverthorne
illustrated by Mike Keepness
translated by Randy Morin, Jean Okimāsis & Arok Wolvengrey

Your Nickel's Worth Publishing
Regina, Saskatchewan

Honouring the Buffalo: a Plains Cree Legend
Text © Ray Lavallee and Judith Silverthorne, 2014; Illustrations © Mike Keepness, 2014
All rights reserved.

Great care has been taken to craft a story with accurate historical information, context, and language. Any mistakes or misrepresentations fall solely on the writer and the interpretation of research, for which I humbly apologize.

Many thanks to Ray Lavallee, Mike Keepness, Randy Morin, Jean Okimāsis, Lori Saigeon, Jeff Sawatzky, Cindy Scheer, Evelyn Siegfried, Arok Wolvengrey and Gregory Younging.

Buffalo artifacts courtesy of the Royal Saskatchewan Museum and Kakwa Crafts.
Photography by Sawatzky Studios.
Educational guide by Lori Saigeon.
Design by Heather Nickel.

Job #: 209132
Printed and bound in Canada by Friesens Printers.
Production made possible with the support of Creative Saskatchewan.

Library and Archives Canada Cataloguing in Publication

Silverthorne, Judith, author
     Honouring the buffalo : a plains Cree legend = Ēwako ōma ohci paskwāwi-mostos kā-kistēyimiht : nēhiyaw-ācimowin / written by Judith Silverthorne ; illustrated by Mike Keepness ; as told by Ray Lavallee, Wisdom Keeper ; translated by Randy Morin, Arok Wolvengrey & Jean Okima¢sis.

Text in English and Cree; translated from the Cree.
ISBN 978-1-927756-33-1 (pbk.)

     1. Cree Indians—Folklore. 2. Bison—Folklore. 3. Folklore—Canada. I. Keepness, Mike, 1981-, illustrator II. Silverthorne, Judith. Honouring the buffalo. III. Silverthorne, Judith. Honouring the buffalo. Cree. IV. Title. V. Title: Ēwako ōma ohci paskwāwi-mostos kā-kistēyimiht.

E99.C88S44813 2015   j398.2089'97323   C2014-906904-9

Published by Your Nickel's Worth Publishing, Regina, SK.

February 2015

ENVIRONMENTAL BENEFITS STATEMENT

Your Nickel's Worth Publishing saved the following resources by printing the pages of this book on chlorine free paper made with 10% post-consumer waste.

TREES	WATER	ENERGY	SOLID WASTE	GREENHOUSE GASES
1	552	1	37	101
FULLY GROWN	GALLONS	MILLION BTUs	POUNDS	POUNDS

Environmental impact estimates were made using the Environmental Paper Network Paper Calculator 3.2. For more information visit www.papercalculator.org.

FSC
www.fsc.org
MIX
Paper from responsible sources
FSC® C016245

PREFACE

I am honoured that Ray Lavallee chose to impart this legend of the buffalo to me and allowed me to share the story in printed book form. Presenting the story in the Plains Cree language (Y dialect) is a vital part of this project, and I am grateful for the skilled translations of Randy Morin and expert editors Arok Wolvengrey and Jean Okimāsis, who have been integral to the authenticity and appropriateness of this work.

The vibrant paintings created by Michael Keepness to accompany the story are representative of the old way of life and the many uses of the buffalo that once roamed in plenty on the prairies. Through the Creator, buffalo gave themselves as a gift for the sustenance and survival of the Plains Cree People *(nēhiyawak)*.

Although the term "bison" is preferred for scientific purposes, both "buffalo" and "bison" are widely used and accepted as interchangeable names for this important North American bovid. The word "buffalo" serves as a reminder of how lives on the Great Plains were once lived, free and in harmony with nature. For me, "buffalo" evokes honour and acknowledges this magnificent creature's gifts to the Indigenous Peoples of the Plains.

In thanks,
Judith Silverthorne

"Mosōm, why do we honour the buffalo skull at our ceremonies?" the grandson asked his grandfather. They stood looking at a buffalo display in a museum.

"The Buffalo were once great creatures that Our People relied on for survival," the grandfather answered.

"Why the buffalo?" asked the grandson.

Grandfather invited his grandson to sit on a bench beside him. "A long time ago, Our People came from the Northern Woodlands to the Great Plains looking for food," Grandfather said. "They saw that the Buffalo lived in harmony with Mother Earth the same as Our People did."

"Weren't there other animals too?" asked the grandson.

"Yes, Nōsisim, there were other large and small animals that were useful, but the Buffalo was valued above them all."

"Tell me more, Mosōm," said the grandson.

"At first Our Ancestors did not know much about this huge creature that roamed the prairies or how to hunt it."

"I don't know anything about them either," said the grandson. "I have never seen a real one."

mosōm [moo SOHM]* or [moo SHOHM]*: "grandfather."
nōsisim [NOH sim] or [NOH sis sim]: "grandson."

* pronounced like the "oo" in "book."

"mosōm, tānēhki ōma māna kā-kihcēyihtamahk paskwāwi-mostos mistikwān ēkotawahk kā-mawimoscikēyahk?" ōsisimimāw kakwēcimēw omosōma. ē-ka-kanawāpahtahkik paskwāwi-mostoswa wiyascikēwina ita kayāsi-kīkwaya kā-kanawēyihcikātēki.

"kayās mētoni kī-kihcēyihtākosiwak paskwāwi-mostoswak ayis kitayisiyinīminawak ē-kī-aspēyimototawācik ka-pimācihocik," itwēw omosōmimāw.

"tānēhki māka paskwāwi-mostos?" itwēw ōsisimimāw.

ēkota ohci kā-kakwēcimāt ka-wītapimikot ōsisima. "kayās kitayisiyinīminawak ōki sakāhk kīwētinohk ē-kī-pē-ohtohtēcik paskwāhk ē-takohtēcik ē-nitonahkik mīciwin," omosōmimāw itwēw. "ē-kiskēyihtahkik paskwāwi-mostos pa-pēyāhtak ē-wīci-pimātisīmimāt okāwīmāw-askīwa pēyakwan tāpiskōc kitayisyinīminawak."

"namōy cī kotakak pisiskiwak kī-ihtakowak?" kakwēcihkēmow nāpēsis.

"tāpwē, nōsisim, kotakak kī-ayāwak ē-māh-misikiticik ēkwa ē-apisīsisicik pisiskiwak ē-āpacihihcik māka paskwāwi-mostos kī-mistakisow ispīhci kotaka."

"kēyāpic wīhtamawin, mosōm," itēw omosōma ōsisimimāw.

"nistam namōya mistahi kī-kiskēyimēwak ōhi kā-misikitiyit pisiskiwa kā-papāmācihoyit paskwāhk ahpō tānisi ka-isi-nōcihācik."

"namōya nīsta nikiskēyimāwak," itwēw ōsisimimāw. "namōya wīhkāc nōhci-wāpamāw ē-pimātisit."

The grandfather rose and took his grandson by the hand. "Come, I will tell you the story about the Buffalo, the Paskwāwimostos, and how we came to honour them," he said.

They rode in Grandfather's car until they left the city far behind and were deep in the countryside. Grandfather stopped the car on a gravel road beside a strong barbed-wire fence surrounding a huge expanse of wind-swept prairie.

As they got out of the car, the grandson asked, "What is this place, Mosōm?"

"You will see, Nōsisim," said Grandfather.

He led his grandson through a gate. They walked across the rolling prairie rich with tall grasses, mint and wildflowers until they came to the top of a rise.

"Why are we here?" asked the grandson. He couldn't see anything but a vast stretch of undulating prairie below them.

"Keep watching," said Grandfather. He pointed towards black specks in the distance.

Grandfather lowered himself to the ground and quietly gazed across the wide-open land. The grandson settled beside him. After some moments, his grandfather began the story of the Buffalo.

omosōmimāw ati-pasikōw ēkota ohci sakicihcēnēw ōsisima. "āstam kika-wīhtamātin paskwāwi-mostos-ācimowin ēkwa tānēhki kā-kihcēyimāyahkik," itwēw omosōmimāw.

pimipayiwak omosōmimāw otāpānāskohk, wāhyaw nakatamwak kihci-ōtēnaw, paskwāhk takopayiwak.

omosōmimāw nakinēw otāpānāskwa cīki pīwāpiskosi-mēnikan ita mētoni ē-paskwāyik, ōsisima itwēyiwa, "tānitē ōma, mosōm?

"kika-wāpahtēn, nōsisim," itwēw omosōmimāw.

ati-sāpohtēwak nakānikanihk. paskwāhk pimohtēwak mistahi maskosiya, amisko-wīhkwaskwa ēkwa wāpikwaniya ē-ohpikiyiki isko kā-takohtēcik tahkohc ispacināsihk.

"tānēhki ōma ōta kā-ayāyahk?" kakwēcihkēmow ōsisimimāw. ma kīkway ē-wāpahtahk tēpiyāhk piko misi-paskwāw nīhcāyihk ita kā-nīpawicik.

"āhkami-ay-itāpi," itwēw omosōmimāw. itwahwēw wāhyaw kīkwāsa ē-kaskicēsisiyit.

omosōmimāw ati-nahapiw pa-pēyāhtak ay-itāpiw akāmi-paskwaskīhk. ōsisima pē-wītapimikow. kētahtawē omosōma kā-māci-ācimoyit paskwāwi-mostos-ācimowin.

paskwāwi-mostos [pus KWOW moos toos]*: "buffalo"
* pronounced like the "oo" in "book."

One day, Buffalo said to the Creator, "I see the two-leggeds have come to the plains and need assistance to live. I would like to help them."

"What will you do for them, Buffalo?" asked the Creator.

"I will give them myself," said Buffalo. "I will let them use every part of my body, as all are equal. They will have shelter, food, clothing and many other things to aid in their survival."

"Tell me how you will do this," said the Creator.

pēyakwāw ēsa paskwāwi-mostos itēw kisē-manitowa, "niwāpamāwak onīsokātēwak ē-pē-takwācihocik paskwāhk ēkwa ē-nitawēyihtahkik ka-wīcihikowisicik. ninōhtē-wīcihāwak."

"kīkwāy ē-wī-nitawi-itōtamawacik, paskwāwi-mostos?" kakwēcimēw kisē-manitow.

"nika-miyāwak niya," itwēw paskwāwi-mostos. "nika-pakitināwak ka-āpacihtācik piko kīkway niyawihk ohci, ayis kahkiyaw ōma ē-wāhkōhtoyahk. ka-kī-ayāwak ita ka-wīkicik, mīciwin, ayiwinisa ēkwa mihcēt kotaka kīkwaya ka-wīcihikocik ka-pimātisicik."

"wīhtamawin tānisi ē-wī-isi-itōtamån ōma." ēsa itwēw kisē-manitow.

Buffalo started to name his body parts.

"They will use my **hair** and **wool** for halters, ropes, and for stuffing saddle pads, pillows, cushions, and even dolls for the young two-leggeds to play with. As well, they will make headdresses, ornaments, bracelets, hairpieces, and medicine balls. My **fur** is also good for blankets, saddle covers, halters, and for making gloves and lining moccasins to keep their hands and feet warm in the cold winter. The **skin** of my hind leg is already pre-shaped for moccasins or boots.

"They will eat my **meat** and my **organs** so that they will not starve. My flesh may be eaten raw, or it may be boiled or roasted. The rest will be dried to make jerky and pemmican with fat berries and nuts or seeds."

"I see you have many uses for your body," said the Creator.

"There is more," said Buffalo.

paskwāwi-mostos māci-wīhtam kahkiyaw kīkwaya kā-ayāt wiyawihk.

"ka-āpacihtāwak **nēscakāsa** ēkwa **nipīwaya** ohci pīminahkwāna ēkwa yōski-tēhtapiwina, aspiskwēsimowina, yōskapiwina, ēkwa ahpō mīna awāsisihkānisa ka-mētawākēcik nīsokāt osk-āyisak. ayahk mīna ka-osīhtāwak mīkwan-astotina, wawēsīhcikana, kispisona, mēscakās-wawēsīhcikana ēkwa pākāhtowāna maskihkiya ohci. **nipīway** ōma mīna ē-miywāsik ohci akohpa, aspapiwin-akwanahikana, ayapihkwēpicikana ēkwa ka-osīhihcik astisak ēkwa pahkēkinwēskisina ka-kīsōnikocik ocihcīwāhk ēkwa ositiwāhk māna kā-pipohk. **nasakay** ohci nāway niskātihk āsay kwēyāci-osīhcikāsow tāpiskōc pahkēkinwēskisina ahpō kinwāpēkaskisina.

"ka-mīciwak **niwiyāsim** ēkwa **nitatāmiyawa**, ēkosi ēkā ka-nipahāhkatosocik. niwiyāsim ka-kī-mīcināniwan ē-askipohk ahpō ka-kī-pakāhcikātēw ahpō ka-kī-nawacīnāniwan. kahkiyaw kotaka ka-kī-pāsikātēwa ka-osīhtāhk kahkēwakwa ēkwa pimīhkān ē-takonamihk mīnisa ahpō pakānisak.

"niwāpahtēn mistahi kīkwaya ka-isi-āpacihcikātēk kiyawihk," itwēw kisē-manitow.

"kēyāpic kīkwaya," itwēw paskwāwi-mostos.

"My insides that are not used for food are good for many other purposes too. My **tongue** is the best part of the meat to eat, but the rough side will also be a good hairbrush. My **bladder** is useful for sinew, quill pouches and small medicine bags. My **scrotum** can be used to make rattles and small pouches. My **paunch** and **large intestine** will line buckets, cups, basins, and dishes so they do not leak. And my **gall** can be used for yellow paints to decorate many things.

"My four-chambered **stomach** has a lining that can be used for containers and buckets to carry and store water, for cooking vessels, and for cups and dishes. The **content** of my first stomach will help cure frostbite and skin diseases, and provide a base for mixing paint.

"kīkwaya ēkā kā-āpacihcikātēki ohci mīciwin ka-kī-pītosi-āpacihcikātēwa mīna. **nitēyiniy** ē-māwaci-miywāsik ka-mīcihk, māka kā-maskawāk ka-kī-āpacihcikātēw ka-sīkahohk. **nisikīwi-wīhkway** ka-kī-āpacihcikātēw ohci asapāp, kawiyak maskimocisa ēkwa mīna ē-apisāsiki maskihkiy maskimocisa. **nitisiwayak** ka-kī-āpacihcikāsowak ka-osīhihcik ohci sīsīkwanak ahpō ē-apisāsiki maskimocisa. **nitatāmiyawa** ka-kī-āpacihcikātēwa ka-astāhk askihkohk, minihkwākanihk, kāsīhkwēwiyākanihk, ēkwa oyākana ēkā ka-ohcikawiki. ēkwa **niwīsopīm** ka-kī-āpacihcikātēw ohci ka-osīhtāhk osāwi-sisopēkahikan ka-wawēsīhcikātēki mihcēt kīkwaya.

"ninēwo-**mataya** ayāwa pīhtwēkinikan ka-āpacihcikātēki maskimota ēkwa askihkwak nipiy ka-kwāpikēhk ēkwa ka-nahascikātēk, ahpō piminawasow-askihkwak ēkwa minihkwākana ēkwa oyākana. **kīkway anima kā-asiwatēk** anita nistam natāhk ka-kī-sisopēhikātēw ita awiyak ē-āhkwacit mīna nanātohk masakay āhkosiwina ēkwa sisopēhikanihk.

"My **hide** will provide shelter, clothing, bedding and other objects," Buffalo continued to explain.

"My **untanned hide** will be made into moccasin soles, armbands, belts, caps and headdresses for the two-leggeds to wear. They will also use it to make buckets, bullet pouches, ropes, containers, knife sheaths, straps, and thongs.

"**nipahkēkinom** ka-kī-āpacihcikātēw ka-osīhtāhk ita ka-wīkihk, ayiwinisa ēkwa kotaka kīkwaya," paskwāwi-mostos ē-āhkami-wīhtahk.

"**nipahkēkinom** ēkā kā-kīsinikātēk ka-osīhtāwak pahkēkinwēskisini-tahkoskākana, mispitonahpisona, pakwahtēhona, astotina ēkwa mīkwan-astotina onīsokātēwak ka-kikiskahkik. ka-āpacihtāwak mīna ka-osīhtācik askihkwa, mōswasiniy-maskimota, pīminahkwāna, asiwacikana, pīhcihkomāna, āniskohpicikana, ēkwa tahkopicikana."

"For the horses they will ride in pursuit of me, they will make horse masks, harnesses, cinches, stirrups, saddles, saddle blankets shields, lariats, and forehead ornaments. They will make mortars and parfleches, and use my **hide** for bull boats and shrouds to honour their dead.

"When they are hurt or injured, the two-leggeds will make splints and medicine bags. Winter robes will make them comfortable in the cold and snowshoes will help them get around in the deep snow. For their ceremonies, they will use my hide to craft drums and drumsticks, rattles, and masks.

"anihi misatimwa kā-tēhtapicik ka-nawaswāsicik, ka-osīhtamawēwak misatim-mihkwākanihkāna, wiyahpicikana, sīhcipayihcikana, tāpiskoskācikana, aspapiwina, aspapiwin-akohpa, nakahāskwāna, pīminahkwāna, ēkwa mistikwān wawēsīhcikēwina. ēkwa ka-āpacihtāwak **nipahkēkinom** nanātohk ōhi ta-isi-kāh-kihcēyimācik kā-pōni-pimātisiyit otayisiyinīmiwāwa.

"kīspin wīsakēyihtamwak ahpō wīsakisinwak, onīsokātēwak ka-osīhtāwak māh-mīnopitamākana ēkwa maskihkiy maskimota. pipon-ayiwinisa ka-miyo-kīsōskākowak tahkāyāyiki ēkwa asāma ka-wīcihikwak ka-papāmohtēcik timikoniyiki. ēkwa otisīhcikēwiniwāwa, ka-āpacihtāwak nipahkēkinom ka-osīhācik mistikwaskihkwa ēkwa pakamahamākana, sīsīkwana, ēkwa mihkwākanihkāna.

"My **hide** will be flexible when it is tanned, suitable for tipi and sweat lodge covers and liners. The two-leggeds may also use my soft tanned hide to clothe themselves in dresses, leggings, moccasin tops, breechcloths, belts, and shirts. They will also create headdresses for ceremonies and costumes to disguise themselves as they hunt me.

"**nipahkēkinom** kā-kīsinikātēk ka-yōskāw ka-osīhtāhk mīkiwahpēkinwa, matotisānēkinwa ēkwa anāskāna. onīsokātēwak ka-kī-āpacihtāwak niyōski-pahkēkinom ka-postayiwinisēhisocik miskotākaya, mitāsa, pakwahtēhona, ēkwa papakiwayāna. ka-osīhtāwak mīna mīkwan-astotina isīhcikētwāwi ahpō kāso-ayiwinisa ispī kā-pē-nōcihicik.

"Cradles and dolls will be made for the younger two-leggeds, and the women will make tapestries. Pouches and containers will also come in handy, as will bedding belts for when they roll up their possessions and travel from place to place in search of me. They will also be able to use my tanned **hide** to make gun cases and lance covers, quivers, shields, rattles, bridles, backrests, paint bags, and pipe bags for everyday use."

"How will they tan your hide?" asked the Creator.

"My **brains**, which can also be eaten as food, are useful for tanning. My **liver** makes a good tanning agent too."

The Creator said, "I am impressed that you have so many useful parts to help the two-leggeds gain their basic needs."

"Ah, but there is even more of me they can use," said Buffalo.

"askotāskopisona ēkwa awāsisihkānisa ka-osīhtamawēwak kā-osk-āyiwiyit nīsokācisa, ēkwa iskwēwak ka-osīhtāwak wawēsīhcikēwi-akohpa. maskimocisa ēkwa asiwacisa ka-miyo-āpatanwa mīna tahkopicikanēyāpiya ka-tihtipiwēpitahkik piko kīkway sipwēyācihotwāwi ka-nitawi-nitonawicik. ka-āpacihtāwak mīna **nipahkēkinom** ohci aspikinākana ēkwa cīkahikwān-akwanahikana, pīhtatiwānak, nakahāskwāna, sīsīkwana, mīnoskwēpicikana, aspatāskopisowina, sisopēhikan maskimota, ēkwa ospwākan maskimota tāpitāw ka-āpacihtāhk.

"tānisi māka kē-isi-atisahkik kipahkēkinom?" ē-kakwēcihkēmot kisē-manitow.

"**nītihp**, ka-mīciwak mīna ēkoni, miywāsinwa ka-pahkēkinohkēhk. **niskon** mīna ē-āpacihtāhk kā-pahkēkinohkēhk.

kisē-manitow itwēw, "tāpwē nitakahkēyihtēn piko kīkway kā-wīhtaman ē-ayāyan kiyawihk ka-isi-wīcihacik onīsokātēwak ka-pimātisicik.

"ā, māka kēyāpic ayiwāk nitayān kīkwaya ka-āpacihtācik," itwēw paskwāwi-mostos.

20

"My **bones** can be used for tools and weapons so that the two-leggeds might hunt and preserve me for their needs. Spear handles, knives, riding whips, paintbrushes, pipes, splints, shovels, and arrow strengtheners will be made for use in their everyday lives. My bones will also make good saddle trees, part of the harness that fits across the back of a horse or dog to pull and carry whatever they need. To defend themselves, they will use my bones to make war clubs.

"My **tibia** and other bones can be used for awls, fleshers and brushes. My **heel bones** will help to make billet straps.

"My **ribs** will make arrowheads and scrapers or fleshing tools. They will also use my ribs as dance sticks and runners on sleds so they can haul goods, and for the young two-leggeds to play with in the summer.

"My **shoulder blades** will make good hoes and runners for winter sledges and sleds. The young two-leggeds will also use my **bones** for toys and game dice. All can paint on my bones and make carvings of them for decorations and use in their ceremonies.

"**niskana** ka-kī-āpacihcikātēwa ohci āpacihcikana ēkwa nōtinikēwi-āpacihcikana ka-ohci-nōcihicik onīsokātēwak ēkwa ka-kahkēwakohkēcik niya. cīstahikanāhtikwa, mōhkomāna, tēhtapiwi-pasastēhikana, sisopēkahikana, ospwākana, māmīnopitamākana, wātihkākanak, ēkwa atos-sōhkipicikana ka-osīhcikātēwa tahto-kīsikāw ka-āpacihtācik. niskana mīna ka-miyo-osīhtāwak aspapiwināhtikwa, ēwako kā-āpacihtācik wiyahpicikan ka-ocipitamiyit mīna ka-pimowatāyit misatimwa ahpō atimwa. niskana ka-āpacihtāwak ta-osīhtācik pakamākana ka-nātamāsocik.

"**niskātikan** ohci ēkwa kotaka oskana ka-kī-āpacihcikātēwa ohci pakonēhikana, mātahikana, ēkwa sisopēkahikana. **nahkwanikana** ka-kī-wicihikowak ka-osīhtācik aniskohpicikana.

"**nispikēkana** ka-ohci-osīhihcik atosak ēkwa mīna kāskahikana ahpō mātahikana. ka-āpacihtāwak mīna nispikēkana ka-osīhtācik nīmihito-mistikwa ēkwa sīkwāpāna otāpānāsk ohci ēkosi ka-āwacitāpēcik mispoki ēkwa oski-nīsokātisak ka-mētawākēcik nīpihki.

"**nitīhiyak** ka-miyo-āpacihāwak kā-ayahikākēhk ēkwa sīkwāpāna piponi-ocipicikana ahpō sōskwaciwākana ohci. oski-nīsokātisak ka-āpacihtāwak **niskana** mētawākana ēkwa ka-pakēsēhk. kahkiyaw kā-kī-masinahipēhikēwak niskanihk ēkwa ka-wiyihkotamwak ka-wawēsīhcikākēcik ēkwa ka-āpacihtācik otisīhcikēwiniwāhk.

"They will use my **horns** for cups, ladles and spoons, for powder horns, fire carriers, signals, and for headdresses and toys. When they take the caps off my horns to make arrow points, I will whisper to them about medicines to heal themselves.

"My **sinews** are for glue, bow strings, arrow ties, cinches and thread, and can also be used as snowshoe webbing. My **hooves**, **feet** and **dewclaws** can be used to make glue, rattles, spoons, and tools.

"ka-āpacihēwak **nitēskana** ohci minihkwākana, kwāpahikana ēkwa ēmihkwāna, pīhcipihkwānak, iskotēw tahkonikana, wāpahcikana, ēkwa mīkwan-astotina ēkwa mētawākana. mayaw kēcikonātwāwi nitēskana ta-kīskiswēwak ita kā-māwaci-wawiyēsiyit ka-osīhtācik atosa, nika-kīmwān ta-wīhtamawakik maskihkiya ka-ohci-nanātawihisocik.

"**nitastinwān** ohci ākoskawahcikan, ahcāpahciya, atos pīminahkwāna, sīhcipayihcikana, asapāp ēkwa mīna kā-kī-āpacihāw ka-osīhtāhk ātimana. **nimahkikasāna (nisita)** ēkwa **nicihcina** ka-kī-āpacihcikātēwa ka-osīhtāhk ākoskawahcikan, sīsīkwanak, ēmihkwānak, ēkwa nanātohk āpacihcikana.

24

"My **blood** will be used in soups, puddings and paints. They will use my **fat** for tallow to make candles, and for soap, cosmetic aids, and hair grease. Necklaces and ornamentation will be made from my **teeth**.

"My **tail** will be used for medicine switches, fly brushes, switches, and outer tipi and lodge decorations. And even my **dung** has purpose for ceremonial smoking, fuel for cooking fires and sending signals. The two-leggeds will also find that it makes good diaper powder, toys and jewelry. They will use my **beard** for ornamentation on weapons and dolls, or for apparel such as mittens."

"**nimihkom** ka-āpacihcikātēw ohci mīcimāpoya, mīciwina, ēkwa sisopēhikanihk. ka-āpacihtāwak **niwiyin** ohci wasaskocēwinisa, ēkwa kisīpēkinikan, wawēsī-tōminikana ēkwa mēscakāsi-pimiy. tāpiskākanak ēkwa wawēsīhcikanak ka-kī-osihāwak **nīpita** ohci.

"**nisoy** ohci ka-kī-osihcikātēwa pasastēhikana, ōcēs pasastēhikana, ēkwa wawēsīhcikana mīkiwahpihk wayawītimihk ēkwa pīhc-āyihk. ahpō **nimēyi** mīna āpacihcikātēw miyahkasikēwin, ka-pōnikātēk kā-piminawasohk iskotēw, ēkwa kā-pīpōtawēhk. onīsokātēwak mīna ka-kiskēyihtamwak nimēyi ē-miywāsik kā-pēkisātisocik oskawāsisak, mētawākana ēkwa wawēsīhowina. ka-āpacihtāwak mīna **nimōtay** ka-wawēsīhtāhk nīmāskwāna ēkwa ka-wawēsihihcik awāsisihkānak ahpō astisak."

"You seem to have everything necessary for their daily lives," said the Creator. "You will give them shelter, food and clothing, and provide tools, weapons and utensils."

"There will be no waste," Buffalo said.

"How will the two-leggeds know where to find you?" the Creator asked.

"They will offer respectful gifts to one of their Wise Old Ones, who will pray and ask for directions to the most healthy of us.

"Before they leave to search for me, the two-leggeds must bless their hunting tools, horses and everything that they will use in the hunt. As soon as they make a successful kill, they will eat a raw piece of my **liver** and put little bits of my body around the area. As they do this, they will give thanks for all the gifts the Creator bestows on them every day.

"Although sometimes they will eat my **eyes**, they must also preserve part of one so that the Wise Old Ones will be able to 'see' Buffalo in the future whenever the two-leggeds are in need."

"piko kīkway ēsa kitayān tahto-kīsikāw ka-pimācihikocik," itwēw kisē-manitow. "ka-miyāwak ita ka-wīkicik, mīciwin, ayiwinisa, ēkwa nanātohk āpacihcikana."

"nama kīkway ka-wēpīnikātēw," itwēw paskwāwi-mostos.

"tānisi māka kē-isi-miskāskik onīsokātēwak?" ē-kakwēcihkēmot kisē-manitow.

"ka-miyēwak mēkiwina kā-kihcēyimācik pēyak okēhtē-ayimiwāwa, ka-kākīsimoyit ka-kakwēcihkēmoyit tānitē ka-miskākoyāhkik niyanān kā-māwaci-miyw-āyāyāhk."

"pāmwayēs sipwēhtētwāwi ka-nitawi-nitonawicik, piko onīsokātēwak ka-miyāhkasahkik piko kīkway kā-wī-āpacihtācik kā-wī-mācīcik: onīmāskwāniwāw, otēmiwāwa, ēkwa kahkiyaw kīkway. mayaw minahotwāwi piko ka-mīcicik, ka-askipocik niskon ēkwa pikw īta ka-papāmastācik apisīs niyaw kā-pīwipitahkik misiwē ita kā-pahkisiniyān. mēkwāc omisi ē-ay-itōtahkik, ka-nanāskomowak piko kīkway kā-miyikocik kisē-manitowa tahto-kīsikāw.

"āta āskaw ka-mīciwak niskīsikwa, piko tāpwē ka-iskonahkik apisīs ohci pēyak ēkosi kā-mamāhtāwisicik kēhtē-ayak 'kē-wāpamācik' paskwāwi-mostoswa ōtē nīkānihk niyōhtēpayitwāwi."

"I have one final question," said the Creator. "How will the two-leggeds honour your abundant gifts?"

Buffalo answered, "The two-leggeds will consider my **skull** sacred. They will decorate it for use in ceremonies and my **bones** will be prayer objects. They will also use my skull in rituals like the Sun Dance, Rain Dance and in Medicine Prayers."

The Creator said, "I am well pleased, and because of your great sacrifices, the two-leggeds may address me through you."

"Thank you for this honour, Creator," said Buffalo.

"You have planned your offerings well, Buffalo," said the Creator. "Now we must speak of the future."

"I know the day will come when I will be no more," Buffalo said, dropping his head.

"Yes," said the Creator, "but even when you are gone, the two-leggeds will honour you for all that you have sacrificed and all that you gave for their survival. They will continue to give thanks for receiving your gifts and for ALL the gifts of life every day."

"nitayān pēyak kīkway iskwēyāc ē-nōhtē-kakwēcimitān," itwēw kisē-manitow. "tānis īsi onīsokātēwak ka-kī-kihcēyihtamwak kimēkiwina?"

paskwāwi-mostos omisi kā-itwēt, "onīsokātēwak ka-mamāhtāwēyihtamwak **nistikwānikan**. ka-wawēsīhtāwak ka-āpacihtācik mawimoscikētwāwi ēkwa **niskana** kākīsimowicihcikana ēkoni. ka-āpacihtāwak nistikwānikan nipākwēsimotwāwi ēkwa kākīsimotwāwi."

kisē-manitow omisi itwēw, "nimiywēyihtēn ēkwa ayisk ē-miyacik kipimātisiwin, onīsokātēwak wiyawāw nika-kī-kākīsimototākwak niya ispīhk kiya kā-āpacihiskik."

"kinanāskomitin ē-miyiyan kihcēyihtamowin, kisē-manitow," itwēw paskwāwi-mostos.

"kwayask kikī-māmitonēyihtēn kimēkiwina, paskwāwi-mostos," itwēw kisē-manitow. "ayahk ēkwa piko ka-pīkiskwātamahk nīkānihk."

"nikiskēyihtēn kētahtawē namōya ōta nika-ayān," itwēw paskwāwi-mostos, ē-tapahtiskwēyit.

"tāpwē," itwēw kisē-manitow, "māka ispīhk namōya ōta ayāyani, onīsokātēwak ka-kihcēyimikwak pikw īsi kā-kī-pē-isi-kitimahisoyan ēkwa mīna piko kīkway kā-kī-miyacik ka-pimātisicik. tāpitawi kika-nanāskomikwak kimēkiwina ohci mīna kahkiyaw pimātisiwi-mēkiwina kā-sawēyimikowisicik tahto-kīsikāw."

Grandfather rose to his feet. "And that is what happened. One day there were no more Buffalo for Our People and life changed, but the story of the Buffalo's gifts to us was passed down by the Old People. We continue to honour the sacred Buffalo Medicine and keep the memories alive."

The grandson turned to his grandfather. "I understand now why the Buffalo skull is important in our ceremonies. They were our way of life."

Grandfather nodded. "The Old People also said there would be a time when the Buffalo needed our help. This is also why we must continue to remember them and offer prayers to their spirit."

"Mosōm, look!" the grandson jumped to his feet and pointed.

The black specks were coming closer at a fast pace.

"Is that Buffalo?" the grandson asked.

"Yes, Nōsisim," said Grandfather. "The Buffalo honour us by coming to greet us."

Grandfather closed his eyes and began to sing a song of thanks in Cree.

omosōmimāw ēkwa pasikōw. "ēkosi anima ē-kī-ispayik. kētahtawē nama kīkway paskwāwi-mostoswa kitayisiyinīminawak ohci ēkwa piko kīkway kī-mēskocipayin, māka paskwāwi-mostos omēkiwina kipē-wīhtamākonawak kēhtē-ayak. kiyānaw kitāhkami-kihcēyihtēnānaw kā-mamāhtāwahk paskwāwi-mostoso-maskihkiy ēkwa ē-kiskisiyahk ācimowina."

ōsisimimāw wīhtamawēw omosōma. "nikiskēyihtēn ēkwa tānēhki kā-kihcēyihtākwahk paskwāwi-mostos mistikwānikan ita kā-mawimoscikēyahk."

omosōmimāw tāpwēhtam. "kēhtē-ayak māna ē-kī-itwēcik kētahtawē paskwāwi-mostos ka-nitawēyimikonaw ka-wīcihāyahk. ēwako ohci mīna ta-kī-āhkami-kiskisitotawāyāhkik ēkwa ka-mawimoscikēyahk otahcahkomiwāwa ohci."

"mosōm, cīst!" ē-pasikōpayihot ōsisimimāw ēkwa ē-itwahikēt.

ē-kaskitēwāyiki kīkwaya ē-pē-sōhkakotēki.

"paskwāwi-mostoswak cī aniki?" ōsisimimāw kakwēcihkēmow.

"tāpwē, nōsisim," itwēw omosōmimāw. "paskwāwi-mostoswak aniki ē-pē-kihcēyimikoyahkok kā-pē-itohtēcik."

omosōmimāw ati-pasakwāpiw ē-māci-nikamot, ē-nanāskomot ē-nēhiyawēt.

The grandson watched the herd pound across the prairie towards them in a swelling cloud of dust. Even before he heard the low rumbling, the ground began to shake.

The herd of buffalo thundered closer and closer. Within moments they would be at the hill upon which they stood. The grandson clutched his grandfather's hand, prepared to run.

Grandfather gripped his grandson's hand, but his voice and song were steady.

The grandson closed his eyes like Mosōm. Even though he didn't know the words, he began to sing softly to the rapidly approaching buffalo.

As the ground trembled harder, and the rumbling drummed in his heart, the grandson took a peek.

Closer and closer the Buffalo came. Quickly he shut his eyes.

Though he was quaking, the grandson sang louder and louder, trying to drown out the thundering roar and his fear. When he could stand it no more, he peeked again.

The herd was almost upon them. As the grandson watched, the massive buffalo herd veered around their hill at the last possible moment in billowing clouds of dust.

ōsisimimāw kanawāpamēw paskwāwi-mostoswa ē-pāpahtāyit ita kā-pē-ohpawakāstaniyik. ē-mōsihtāt askiy ē-māci-nanamipayiniyik, pāmwayēs ē-pēhtawāt paskwāwi-mostoswa.

cāh-cīki ē-pāpahtāyit mitoni ē-matwēpahtāyit. wīpac ka-takopayiyiwa ita kā-nīpawicik tahkohtamatin. ōsisimimāw sakiniskēnēw omosōma ē-wawēyikāpawit ka-sipwēpahtāt.

omosōmimāw sakiniskēnēw ōsisima, sōskwāc pa-pēyāhtak nikamow.

ōsisimimāw pasakwāpiw tāpiskōc omosōma, kiyām āta namōya ē-kiskēyihtahk itwēwina, māci-nikamostawēw paskwāwi-mostoswa ē-pē-sōhkēpahtāyit.

tahk āyiwāk ē-ati-nā-nanamipayiyik askiy, ēkwa ē-ati-misi-nanamipayit otēhihk, ōsisimimāw kīmōtāpiw.

cāh-cīki paskwāwi-mostoswak ē-pāpahtācik; sisikwac pasakwāpiw.

āta ē-nā-nanamipayit, ōsisimimāw ayiwāk sōhki-nikamow, ē-kakwē-kiponahk kisīwēwin ēkwa osēkisiwin. sākōcihikow, ēkosi kī-kīmōtāpiw.

paskwāwi-mostoswak kēkāc takosipayiwak. ōsisimimāw ē-ka-kanawāpamāt paskwāwi-mostoswa sisikwac kwēskipahtāyiwa ita kā-nīpawicik mitoni ē-misi-ohpwēwēskamiyit.

Grandfather's song died away as the last of the main herd thundered past them. The grandson watched an aging buffalo straggle behind the others.

The Old One slowed for a moment and his enormous head swivelled towards them.

Grandfather locked eyes with the great beast.

The grandson held his breath as two pairs of dark brown eyes connected, sharing some message.

A moment later, the Old Buffalo gave a loud snort and wheeled away to catch up to the rest of the herd.

The grandson and his grandfather watched the buffalo pound across the prairie until the ground became still once again and the rumbling fell away into silence.

omosōmimāw onikamowin pōnihtākwaniyiw kā-atimipahtāyit kahkiyaw paskwāwi-mostoswa ita kā-nīpawicik. ōsisimimāw ka-kanawāpamēw pēyak kēhtē-paskwāwi-mostoswa ē-nakatimiht. aciyaw nakīyiwa, ē-kwēskiskwēyiyit ē-kitāpamikocik.

omosōmimāw kanawāpamitowak wiya ēkwa anihi paskwāwi-mostoswa.

ōsisimimāw kī-kakwē-pōni-yēhēw ē-wāpamāt omosōma ēkwa paskwāwi-mostoswa ē-kanawāpamitoyit tāpiskōc kīkway ē-ācimostātocik.

ēkota ohci kā-kēhtē-ayiwit paskwāwi-mostos sisikwac ē-kitot ēkota ohci sipwēpahtāw ē-nawaswātāt kahkiyaw kotaka paskwāwi-mostoswa.

ōsisimimāw ēkwa omosōma kī-kanawāpamēwak anihi paskwāwi-mostoswa ē-matwē-atimipahtāyit isko ispīhk kīhtwām ē-ati-kāmwātahk paskwāhk.

Finally, the grandson spoke. "Mosōm, will you teach me the ways and the songs to honour the Buffalo?" he asked.

"You've already had your first lesson." Grandfather's eyes twinkled.

The grandson laughed. "Yes, but I need lots of practice."

Grandfather smiled. "Grandson, there is always much to learn about Buffalo Medicine."

The grandson slipped his hand into his grandfather's and the two looked over the broad prairie at the buffalo grazing in the distance.

ēkota ohci kā-pīkiskwēt ōsisimimāw. "mosōm, ka-kī-kiskinwahamawin cī tānisi kā-isi-ka-kihcēyimakik paskwāwi-mostoswak, nikamowinihk?"

"āsay kikiskēyihtēn pēyak kīkway." omosōmimāw oskīsikwa ē-wāsēyāyiki.

ōsisimimāw pāhpiw. "tāpwē māka mistahi piko ka-kāh-kociyān."

omosōmimāw pāhpinākosiw. "nōsisim, tāpitawi mistahi kīkwaya ka-kiskēyihtamihk paskwāwi-mostoso-maskihkiy ohci."

ōsisimimāw sakiniskēnēw omosōma ē-kanawāpamācik paskwāwi-mostoswa ē-mīcisoyit wāhyaw paskwāhk.

THINGS MADE FROM BUFFALO

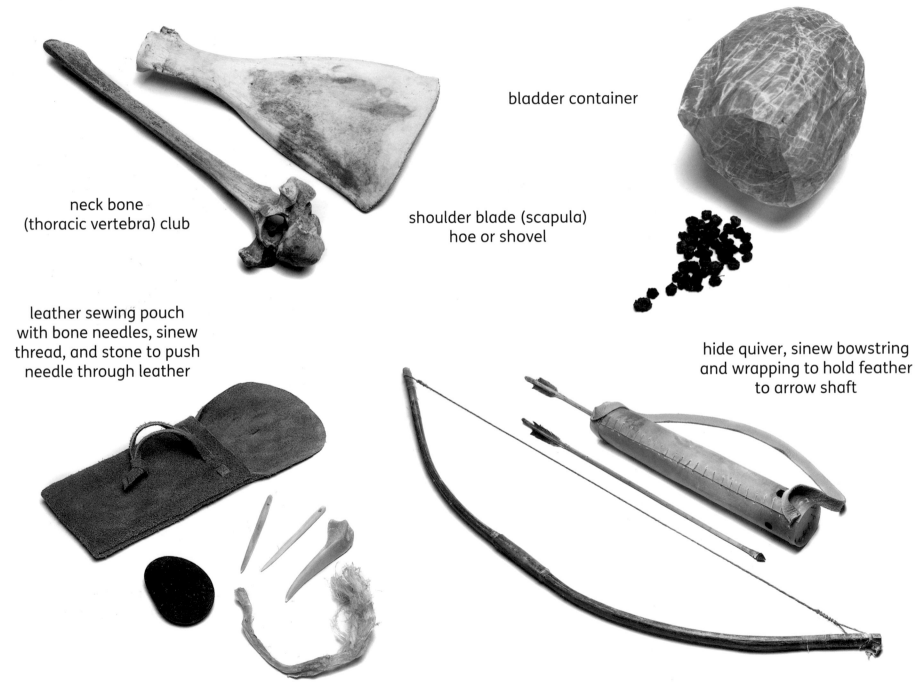

bladder container

neck bone
(thoracic vertebra) club

shoulder blade (scapula)
hoe or shovel

leather sewing pouch
with bone needles, sinew
thread, and stone to push
needle through leather

hide quiver, sinew bowstring
and wrapping to hold feather
to arrow shaft

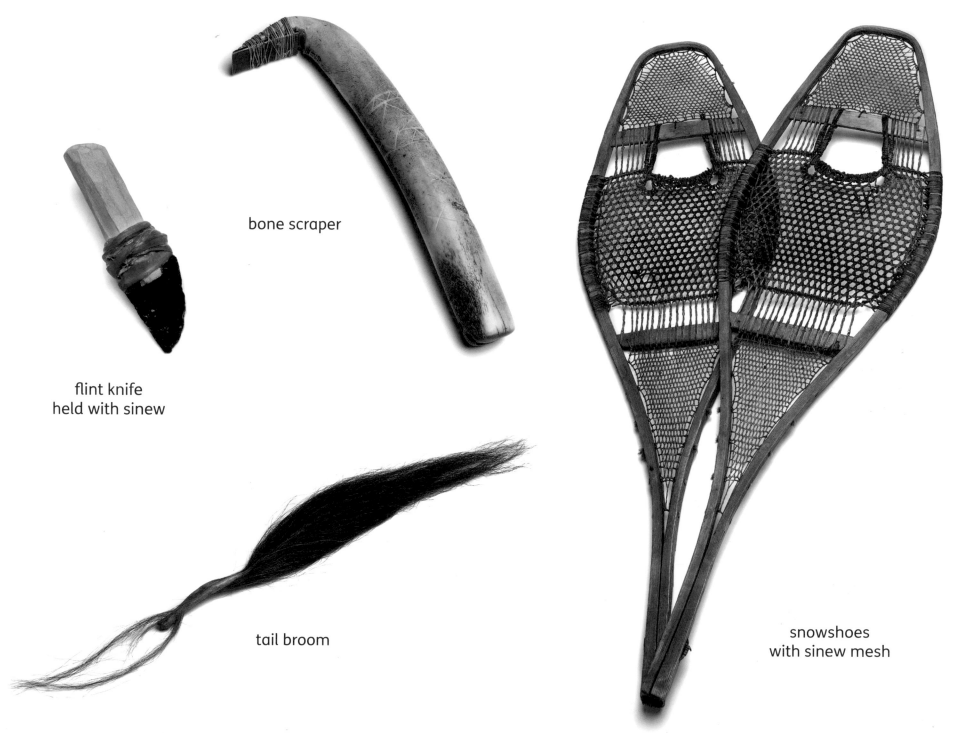

bone scraper

flint knife
held with sinew

tail broom

snowshoes
with sinew mesh

41

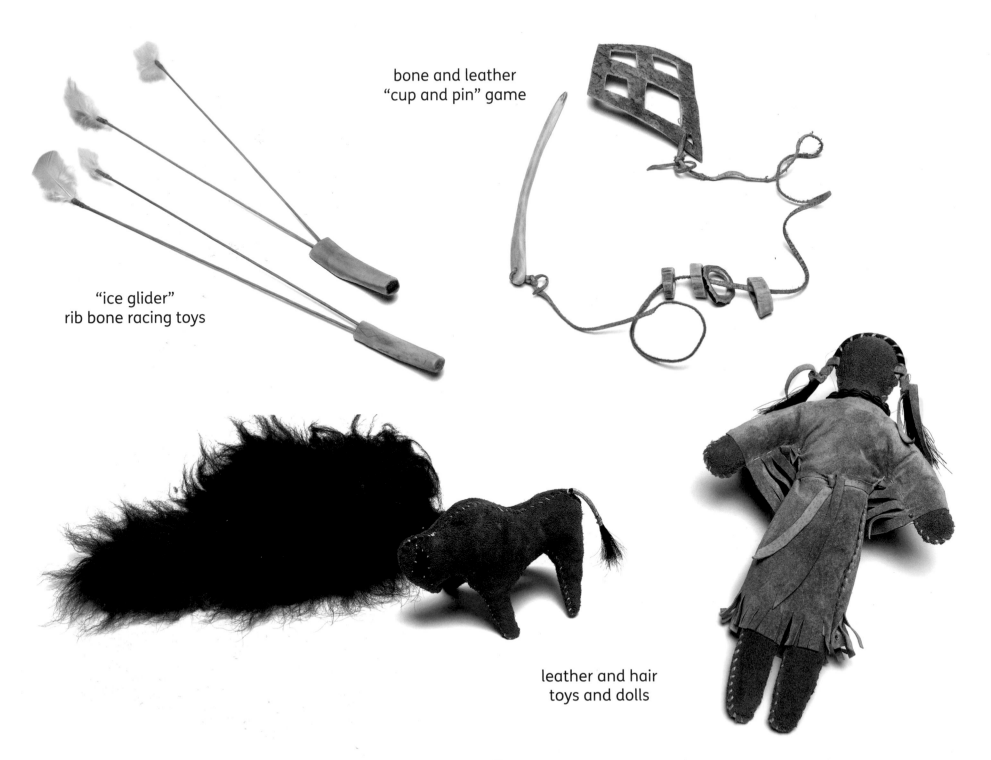

bone and leather
"cup and pin" game

"ice glider"
rib bone racing toys

leather and hair
toys and dolls

leather pouches

rawhide *parfleche*
plain and decorated

43

leather mitts

decorated hide pantcuffs

leather moccasins

decorated hide belt

decorated hide leggings

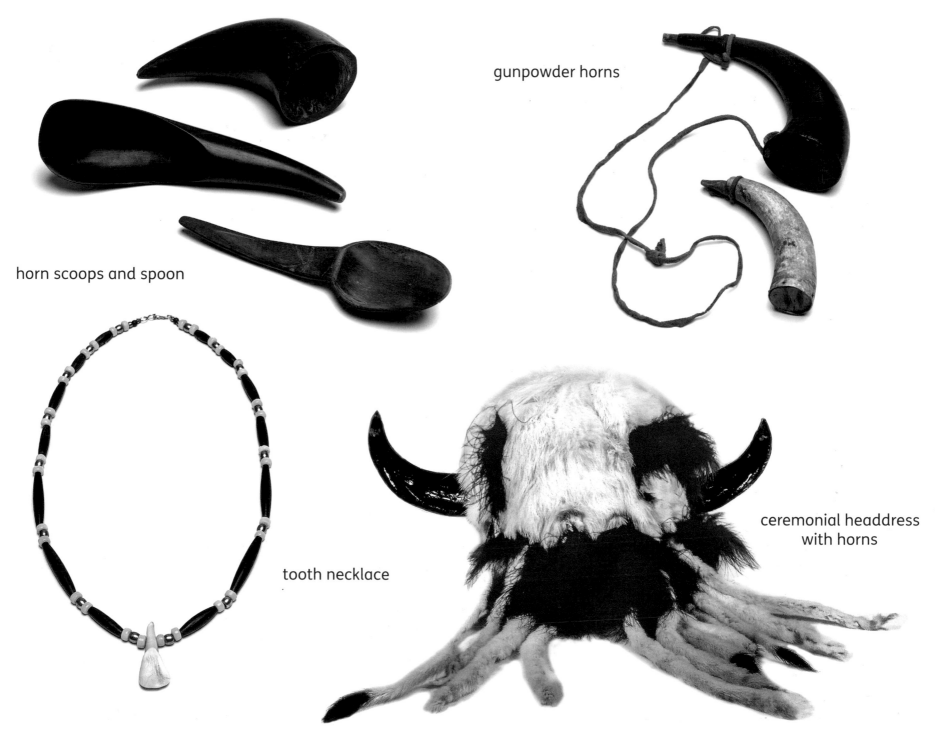

gunpowder horns

horn scoops and spoon

tooth necklace

ceremonial headdress
with horns

WHAT DO YOU KNOW ABOUT THE BUFFALO?

- Buffalo (bison) are the heaviest land animals in North America. Their average weight is 725 kilograms (1,598 lbs).

- Buffalo stand 1.5 to 2 metres (5–6.5 feet) tall at the shoulder and are 2 to 3.5 metres (6.6–11.5 feet) long.

- Buffalo have an average life span of 20-40 years.

- Both the male buffalo (bull) and female buffalo (cow) have a large head, scraggly beard, and sharp, curved horns that can grow to be 61 centimetres (2 feet) long.

- Buffalo can jump vertically up to 1.8 metres (6 feet) and are able to turn quickly and change direction to fight predators.

- They can run up to 65 kilometres (40 miles) per hour for as for as 0.4 kilometres (0.25 miles).

- Buffalo are good swimmers. They float easily, and their head, hump and tail stay above the surface of the water.

- Though buffalo have poor eyesight, their hearing and sense of smell are excellent. Buffalo can smell another animal from about 3 kilometres away.

- Buffalo have a winter coat so thick and well insulated that snow can cover their backs without melting.

- A buffalo's hump is made up of muscle supported by long vertebrae. The strength of these muscles allows them to use their heads like a snowplow when looking for food in winter.

- Buffalo travel far and wide to graze, moving continuously to feed on plains grasses, herbs, shrubs, and twigs as they roam. They regurgitate their food and chew it as cud before digestion.

- Cows lead family groups of buffalo as they roam to graze. For most of the year, the bulls stay on their own or in small groups, but they rejoin the herd during mating season.

- Buffalo eat early in the morning and late in the afternoon, but they are mostly active at dusk and nighttime. During the day, they rest, chew their cud or wallow in dirt.

- Buffalo break up the soil with their hooves, which helps many plant and animal species to flourish.

- Grizzly bears, grey wolves, and cougars still prey on North American buffalo.

- Buffalo are one of the most dangerous animals in North America. In Yellowstone National Park in the United States, three times more people are killed by buffalo than by bears.

- Fossils show that Yellowstone National Park is the only place in the United States that buffalo have lived continuously since prehistoric times.

- For nearly 6,000 years, Indigenous Peoples of the North American plains hunted buffalo by stampeding them over a cliff at Head-Smashed-In-Buffalo Jump in Alberta, Canada.

- An estimated 30 to 50 million buffalo once ranged from northern Canada to northern Mexico, and across the Great Plains from eastern forests to the western Rocky Mountains.

- Loss of habitat due to extensive settlement, the introduction of rifles, and unregulated hunting for buffalo hides and sport deprived Indigenous Peoples of their most important natural asset.To survive, most Indigenous Peoples signed treaties that forced them onto reserves.By 1889, the buffalo population had been reduced to only about 1,100.

- There are approximately 400,000 buffalo in North America today. Only 20,000 are considered wild.

- In Canada, about 5,000 buffalo now roam freely in protected areas in southern and northwest Saskatchewan, northeast British Columbia, and in the Northwest Territories.

EDUCATIONAL GUIDE

GENERAL QUESTIONS

1. What did Plains Cree People use the buffalo for? (Name three uses.)
2. Name three uses for buffalo hide.
3. Name three uses for buffalo bones.
4. Name three uses for buffalo fur.
5. Name three uses for buffalo meat.
6. According to Mosōm, where did the Plains Cree People come from before they moved to the Great Plains?
7. How did the Plains Cree People figure out how to use the buffalo?
8. Why do Plains Cree People preserve part of the buffalo?
9. How do Plains Cree People honour the buffalo and its gifts?
10. Why do the Plains Cree People still honour the buffalo?
11. How do the buffalo honour the People?
12. Why did Mosōm sing to the buffalo?
13. This story is written in English and in Cree. How do written Cree words look different from written English words?

INFERENTIAL QUESTIONS

1. How does this story show Plains Cree People passing on their knowledge?
2. Why did the Old One stop to look at Mosōm?
3. Why did the grandson want to learn the ways and songs to honour the buffalo?
4. Why do you think the story is also written in the Cree language?

SYNTHESIS QUESTIONS

1. What do you think is the most interesting thing made from the buffalo? Why?
2. What item do you think people might still use today?
3. How did it make you feel to read and learn about the Plains Cree People using the buffalo to survive?
4. Why do you think the story is told from the buffalo's point of view?
5. Have you ever been told a story from your culture? Briefly write a story that has been passed on in your family or among your people.
6. The grandson is frightened as the buffalo draw near, but his Mosōm's presence gives him courage and comfort. Retell an experience from your life when you felt brave in a scary situation and why.

7. How would the lives of the Plains Cree People have been different in the past without the buffalo? Choose one item made from the buffalo and imagine what you would use instead.
8. Many people speak two or even more languages, such as English and Cree. Do you think it is important to learn or continue speaking the language of your people, or should you speak only English or French, the official languages of Canada?

RESEARCH QUESTIONS AND ACTIVITIES

1. Buffalo still live in Saskatchewan and other places. Where do they live today?
2. What do buffalo eat?
3. How did the Plains Cree People hunt the buffalo?
4. What other resources did the Plains Cree People use?
5. Many cultures tell stories to explain how things have come to be or how things were in the past or are today. Research another story from another culture and tell what it explains.
6. Choose another animal or plant that is or was used by people. Tell its story from its own point of view, much the way the buffalo told the Creator about its uses. Can you put yourself in that animal or plant's place?
7. Draw a picture of the buffalo. Label the major parts of the buffalo.
8. Cook bison/buffalo burgers or make pemmican.
9. Make a list of objects that are made from one part of the buffalo. Select one object and write a riddle that's a clue to the object's identity. Present your riddle to a partner or your small group or class. See if your classmates can guess what the object is.
10. Draw a web with a part of the buffalo in the middle. In the web, list all the items for which that part is used.
11. Mike Keepness is an amazing artist. Draw and colour or paint your own buffalo hunting or buffalo part scene.
12. Many stories come from other languages. Find someone you know who speaks another language. Write down five words from the other language with their English translations.
13. Some places around southern Saskatchewan are named from Cree words, such as "Pasqua" and "Wascana." Find other places whose names come from other languages. (eg. Ottawa—Anishinaabe).

NOTE: *Honouring the Buffalo: A Plains Cree Legend* meets Social Studies Curriculum Outcomes for Grades 1–6.

RESOURCES

Aboriginal Affairs and Northern Development Canada. "First Nations in Canada." https://www.aadnc-aandc.gc.ca/eng/1307 460755710/1307460872523. Accessed 12/08/2014.

Agriculture in the Classroom. "Saskatchewan History—The First Peoples" and "Saskatchewan History: The First Peoples—The First Nations of the Plains: Family Life, The Children and Duties." http://www.aitc.sk.ca/saskschools/firstnations/index.html. Accessed 12/08/2014.

Alberta Culture and Tourism. "Head-Smashed-In Buffalo Jump World Heritage Site." http://www.history.alberta.ca/headsmashedin. Accessed December 3, 2014.

"American Bison." Wikipedia. http://en.wikipedia.org/wiki/American_bison. Accessed December 3, 2104.

"American Bison." NatureWorks. http://www.nhptv.org/natureworks/americanbison.htm. Accessed December 3, 2014.

Animal Fact Guide. "American Bison." http://www.animalfactguide.com/animal-facts/american-bison. Accessed 12/02/2014.

"Bison." Wikipedia. http://en.wikipedia.org/wiki/Bison. Accessed 12/02/2014.

"Bison antiquus." Wikipedia. http://en.wikipedia.org/wiki/Bison_antiquus. Accessed 12/06/2014.

"Bison Hunting." Wikipedia. http://en.wikipedia.org/wiki/Bison_hunting. Accessed 12/02/2014.

Bison Producers of Alberta. "Prehistoric Human and Bison Relationships on the Plains of North America." Bison Centre. http://bisoncentre.com/index.php/producers-2/resource-library/ibc2000-proceedings/bison-archeology/-prehistoric-human-and-bison-relationships-on-the-plains-of-north-america-. Accessed 12/11/2014.

Canadian Geographic. "Bison Facts Sheet." Kids / Animal Facts. http://www.canadiangeographic.ca/kids/animal-facts/bison.asp. Accessed 12/02/2014.

Canadian History: A Distinct Viewpoint. 'Indian History 1870 – 1879." http://metis-history.info/indian23.shtml. Accessed 12/08/2014.

Canisius College Ambassadors for Conservation. "Bison." http://www.conservenature.org/learn_about_wildlife/prairie/bison.htm. Accessed 12/02/2014.

Daily News Dig. "10 Interesting Facts You Probably Never Knew." http://dailynewsdig.com/interesting-facts. Accessed 12/02/2014.

Defenders of Wildlife. Fact Sheet: Bison. "Basic Facts About Bison." http://www.defenders.org/bison/basic-facts. Accessed 12/02/2014.

Greater Yellowstone Science. "Bison Overview." http://www.greateryellowstonescience.org/download_product/589/0. Accessed 12/04/2014.

Hinterland Who's Who. "North American Bison." http://www.hww.ca/en/species/mammals/north-american-bison.html. Accessed December 3, 2014.

"History of bison conservation in Canada." Wikipedia. http://en.wikipedia.org/wiki/History_of_bison_conservation_in_Canada. Accessed 12/02/2014.

Kohler, Judith. "6 Amazing Facts You Never Knew About Bison." Wildlife Promise. http://blog.nwf.org/2012/02/6-amazing-facts-you-never-knew-about-bison. Accessed 12/02/2014.

Nature Conservancy, The. "Where the Bison Roam." http://www.nature.org/ourinitiatives/regions/northamerica/unitedstates/illinois/explore/where-the-bison-roam.xml. Accessed 12/08/2014.

National Geographic. "American Bison." http://animals.nationalgeographic.com/animals/mammals/american-bison. Accessed 12/02/2014.

National Geographic. "America's Greatest Animals: Bison: The American Legend." http://channel.nationalgeographic.com/wild/videos/bison-the-american-legend. Accessed 12/02/2014.

National Geographic Kids. "American Bison." Animals. http://kids.nationalgeographic.com/content/kids/en_US/animals/american-bison. Accessed 12/02/2014.

Sacred Ground International. "Buffalo and Conservation." http://www.sacredgroundintl.org/conservation.php. Accessed December 3, 2014.

Scribol. "The Near Annihilation of America's Buffalo in Pictures." http://scribol.com/anthropology-and-history/the-near-annihilation-of-americas-buffalo-in-pictures/. Accessed 12/11/2014.

Switch Zoo. Animal Profiles. "Bison." http://switchzoo.com/profiles/bison.htm. Accessed December 3, 2014.

Tatanka: Story of the Bison. "Tatanka: About Bison." http://www.storyofthebison.com/abouttatanka.htm. Accessed 12/08/2014.

The Bison—America's famed icon. "Fascinating Facts About the Bison." http://www.grandcanyonranch.com/the-buffalo-americas-famed-icon. Accessed December 3, 2014.

Wildlife Journal Junior. "American Bison." http://www.nhptv.org/wild/americanbison.asp. Accessed 12/02/2014.

Yellowstone National Park Service. "Yellowstone Bison" http://www.nps.gov/yell/naturescience/bison.htm. Accessed 12/08/2014.

Ray Lavallee is a Wisdom Keeper and Medicine Man from Piapot Cree First Nation who speaks both Cree and Saulteaux, as well as English and some French. He always follows his culture and learned everything he knows from his grandmother, Mrs. Mabel Whitestar, a Medicine Woman from Day Star First Nation. He has travelled throughout North America and to places like Cuba, Germany and Switzerland to share his culture and learn about others.

Judith Silverthorne, a multiple-award winning author, has lived most of her life in Saskatchewan, exploring its culture and history, and revelling in the natural beauty of the prairie landscape, which provides inspiration for many of her books.

Mike Keepness grew up on the Pasqua First Nation, an Aboriginal reserve in southern Saskatchewan. The Qu'Appelle Valley was his childhood playground, a ready source of adventure and new discoveries. To this day he wanders through coulees and hills and spends time by the river, where he receives inspiration—for Mike, nature is a place of prayer, a sanctuary. Being in nature and experiencing it firsthand is the foundation of all his work.

Randy Morin is a teacher/storyteller/musician osci Big River First Nation, Treaty Six area, who lives in Saskatoon with his family. He has a Bachelor of Arts Degree in Indigenous Studies and a Bachelor of Education degree, and a lifetime of traditional Plains Cree teachings. Randy is a strong supporter of maintaining and teaching Cree language and culture, and shares this knowledge and teachings in the classroom as a high school teacher at Oskayak High School in Saskatoon, SK.

Jean Okimāsis was born at White Bear First Nation in southeastern Saskatchewan. As a Cree teacher and curriculum designer, Jean spent twenty years at the Saskatchewan Indian Federated College (now First Nations University of Canada), where she wrote the widely used text, *Cree, Language of the Plains*. She continues to champion Cree language revitalization and literacy through her work and many publications as translator and editor.

Arok Wolvengrey grew up near Saskatoon and became a linguist, specializing in the Cree language through the mentorship of the late Dr. Freda Ahenakew. He compiled the most extensive Cree-English bilingual dictionary, *nēhiyawēwin: itwēwina / Cree: Words*, and is currently head of the Department of Indigenous Languages, Arts and Cultures at First Nations University. He continues to contribute to numerous projects which promote the revitalization of the Cree language, including many online resources.